BJØRN R. LIE

Slush Mountain

SIMPLY READ BOOKS

It's a clear, crisp morning on **Slush Mountain**. There's not a cloud in the sky and the fresh snow shines in the sunlight.

At **Wanderlust Lodge**, the temperature is four below, and the skiing conditions are second to none.

The cross-country trails on **Icicle Ridge** are already crawling with rosy-cheeked skiers. With backpacks full of oranges and chocolate chip cookies, some are slogging up the mountainside, and some are cruising down it.

Others prefer to go off-trail, away from the crowds and long lineups.

The insufferable show-off Bruce "the Spruce" Crampon is ski jumping off the roof of **Lone Wolf Cabin**.

Slush Mountain Ski Resort isn't for the fainthearted. Hardcore downhill skiers fly down the white-knuckle slopes in a flurry of snow and ice. Young daredevils challenge the laws of gravity with death-defying stunts.

On the **Goose Bump Glacier** mogul run, a member of the ski patrol is dealing with a reckless speed demon. Her lift ticket is revoked for dangerous skiing.

However, not everyone is in a hurry.

A young couple is kissing like crazy on the **Chilly Winds Chairlift**, without a care in the world.

Only a short distance away, insults are flying. Two quarrelsome types have decided to settle their differences on the roof of the **Gutsy Pines Gondola**.

" Go back to the bunny hill,
you talentless snowshoe! "
says one.

" Watch your mouth,
you smelly old ski boot! "
cries the other.

Meanwhile, two tough lumberjacks
are ferociously felling trees out in
Sluggerdale Forest.

This is where the wealthy bobsled king,
Christopher Longjohns, plans to
build his controversial log mansion.

Out on **Frostbite Fish Pond**, old "Snow-Blind" Jefferson is fishing through a hole in the ice. So far he's caught a variety of fish, as well as some rusty old cable bindings and a waterlogged ice skate.

Near the top of **Snowplow Summit**, three young mothers are sipping hot chocolate in the midday sun. The view is spectacular, and so is their kids' snow sculpture.

Up on the mountain plateau, the annual **Slush Mountain Rally** is about to kick off. Powerful engines are revving up and the smell of exhaust and motor oil fills the air. The atmosphere is so tense you could cut it with an ice pick.

In the
**Sugar Hill
Ski Jumping
Championship . . .**

Tara Flight has just set
a new world record with
an awe-inspiring leap.

But not everyone is outdoors. Downtown, the humdrum of everyday life goes on as usual.

At **Foothills High School**, a class is learning about a famous race between two explorers to reach the South Pole. Despite the exciting topic, the last lesson of the day feels like a ship locked in ice.

In **Dagny's Boutique**, the world-famous fashion designer is putting the finishing touches on her latest headgear collection. Balaclavas are all the rage this season.

Along **Main Street**,
everyone's eager to get home.

Snowshoe-maker Russel Sprout has just
picked up his kids from kindergarten and barely
avoids the worst of rush hour traffic.

19

A rugged snowmobile gang has gathered outside **Lasse's Grill and Bar**. Their debate about the day's sporting events is heating up over fries and gravy.

In **Black Diamond Lodge**, the after-party is in full swing. The partygoers are slurping warm soup and shamelessly exaggerating their exploits on the slopes.

Back on the **Icicle Ridge** cross-country tracks, a lone skier is still struggling homeward. With one of her skis tugging and the other one slipping, the last few miles are tough going.

As evening falls, the temperature plummets. In the many log cabins around **Backwater Brook**, most everyone is snuggling around their fireplaces or cranking up their wood-burning stoves.

Down in nearby **Powder Valley**, avid bird-watcher
Michael Mittens suddenly spots the extremely rare three-headed
giant hummingbird. Unfortunately, he doesn't have his camera
with him so will never be able to prove he saw it.

In the **Grizzly Guest Chalet**, the Hillarys are enjoying a game of Trivial Pursuit. Young Edward impresses his dad with detailed knowledge about the abominable snowman.

The virtuoso accordion player Johnny Pinetops is entertaining the guests at the **Slopeside Hotel**.

The last tune of the evening, his self-composed "Slush Mountain Waltz," makes even the stiffest skier shake a leg on the dance floor.

Meanwhile, up on the mountainside, the slopes are peaceful and deserted. The stars twinkle in the night sky, and the north wind whistles through the chairlift's cables. It looks like tomorrow will be another glorious day on **Slush Mountain**.

Published in 2016 by Simply Read Books
www.simplyreadbooks.com

Copyright © 2008 Magikon Forlag
www.magikon.no • www.bjornlie.com

Library and Archives Canada Cataloguing in Publication
Lie, Bjorn Rune
[Slapsefjell. English]
Slush mountain / written and illustrated by Bjørn Rune Lie.
Translation of: Slapsefjell.
ISBN 978-1-927018-82-8 (bound)
I. Title. II. Title: Slapsefjell. English.
PZ7.L6325Sl 2015   j839.823'8   C2015-902465-X

This translation has been published
with the financial support of NORLA.

We gratefully acknowledge for their financial support of our
publishing program the Canada Council for the Arts,
the BC Arts Council, and the Government of Canada
through the Canada Book Fund (CBF).

Translated from the original Norwegian by
Dr. John P. Coakley, of Nor-Word Text Services.
Printed in South Korea.
Book design by Heather Lohnes.
10 9 8 7 6 5 4 3 2 1